CHARGED CONNECTIONS

Charged Connections

LILLY LOAR

Widdlepuff Press

Contents

"The family is one of nature's masterpieces."
-George Santayana

Warning!

You are about to enter the magical world of fantasy where logic is thrown out the window and drama and adventure are interlaced into every story.

Chapter 1

Prologue

Ernaline

17 years ago...

I've just been disowned.

The blood drains from my face, and my hands go cold. My father, Gituku, chose my sister Ambrosia to be the next princess—not *me*. He believes I have been corrupted by evil and a want for power. His fear is that under my leadership, only *I* will flourish rather than our entire civilization, the Widdlepuffs. Our great civilization has recently been freed from a corrupt leader seeking to dominate beyond our world. He believes his favorite daughter, my sister, will help heal our planet.

I look up at my father in disbelief. His deep purple eyes gaze down at me impassively.

He is grayer than me. While I have a stark white appearance from head to toe and vibrant lime green eyes, his pallor is granite gray due to his age. My father is nearly 203 years old, which is old, even by our standards. He is finally preparing for when he inevitably passes. But he is making so many wrong choices. First, he ignored the rightful line of succession, and then he kicked me out of my own family!

And then there's my sister, Ambrosia, who looks like me in many ways except for her bright golden eyes—the golden child. Amber, as my father affectionately calls her, squeals in delight, like she has just won the lottery.

We have always been in constant competition, but she has finally won the grand prize. I stalk off, away from my *once* family, already plotting my revenge. I will take the throne because it is my right.

Our planet is shades of gray—Colorless except for our eyes and our powers. The streets, paved with stones, are coated in a fine white dust. The rocks crunch beneath my heavy footsteps, sending puffs of dust into the air. It appears as if I am smoking in anger. Widdlepuffs look on as I stomp down the street, clearly in a temper. Some of them bow. Others look on in horror, already knowing what has happened, but I pay them no mind. I walk directly to my hideout, which is full of fireproof furniture, to let out the heat building inside of me.

I scream and explode into a molten orange fire. The fire soothes my rage and burns my energy. After my fury is spent, I slowly extinguish myself, limb by limb, and slump down in my chair. My lungs fill with the familiar scent of smoke, calming me further. Finally, clear-headed, I stew in my desire for revenge. The path forward is clear.

All I need to do is kill my sister. Then, Father will have no choice but to make me next in line, and I will finally rule our world. *Simple.*

. . .

Guards fill the streets, forcing me to sneak around under the cloak of darkness. Creeping along the roads from my hideout, I head back towards the palace. *I suppose it doesn't count as sneaking back into my home, as I am no longer a part of the family. Now, I am breaking in.*

I ponder this as I enter the castle through a secret door. The silver walls gleam in the faint light of our second moon. The palace was built specifically to capture this moon shine. Banners with our kingdom's symbol, a Widdlepuff skull, drape the hallways. The wind whistles underneath them as if the ancestors are speaking through the walls.

I slink into Ambrosia's room, but unfortunately, she's awake. She screams in terror upon seeing me. She has done the calculations as well as I have, and her fearful eyes tell me she already knows my plan.

Act.

Now.

An internal voice screams at me. Moving fast, I jump her and cover her mouth. I know it's already pointless; her guards were alerted the moment she shrieked.

I take out my knife and, without any remorse, draw the blade across her throat. It glides through skin and blood vessels as easily as softened butter. The guards burst into the room and restrain me using quite a bit of brute force. *Pathetic.*

I am pushed to the ground. My face pressed into the scratchy carpet. The kinder, tender-hearted of the two guards check on my sister. I already know what he will find. She crumpled instantly, gagging on her own blood. I smirk at my handiwork.

. . .

My knees scrape on the cold stone floor as I am presented in front of my father. Unfortunately, not as the future princess like I planned. I am offered— no—given—to my father as a prisoner, a *murderer.* Except my sister hasn't died *yet.* She's still alive, just in critical condition. This fact does nothing to calm my father.

"You are no daughter to me! You are no longer welcome in this family or on this planet ever again! You are banished!" my father bellows. I am disowned AND banished. The last word rings in my ears, repeating itself over and over again. *Banished, banished, banished.*

Before I can even respond, I am placed in cold and constricting handcuffs used to restrain and disable my powers. I am hurried onto a space cruiser. The engine rumbles low beneath my feet as my banishment comes into effect *immediately.*

. . .

Landing on Earth feels like a cruel joke. This planet

is full of loud noises and *color*s. With so much color, my senses are instantly overwhelmed.

I stumble out of the ship in a haze, blinking against the bright sun and vibrant hues. The moment both feet are planted on the ground, the ship immediately flies away, and I am stranded.

I sit down in the field full of little flowers that smell like honey. Somehow, they remind me of my sister and her honey-colored eyes. The grass beneath me is verdant, prickly, and strangely soft beneath my fingertips. This vantage point offers a perfect view of the town below. I observe the inhabitants of my new home for a while.

Robert is the one who found me sitting on the grass.

Chapter 2

Rosalynna

Present day...
"RUN!" I shout to the crowd of onlookers.

"Get them out of here!" I command my brother Ed. He looks at me, his gray eyes, so unlike mine, slightly covered by a brown mop of hair. His eyes silently pleaded with me not to enter the fight. I give him a firm, downward nod so he knows I won't back down. Ernaline has been after us, no, me, for months now. I need to end this once and for all!

I think back to when the situation started. It began typically, like any other ordinary day, but then it spiraled out of my control.

The stress and anxiety of her relentless pursuit push against the walls of my very being, urging me to burst and give up. Doubt creeps in at the edges of my mind, making it hard to focus.

I watch Ed slowly clear the spectators away. He is

trying not to create panic amongst the audience, but the longer they take, I can tell, the faster his facade of calm begins to crumble. He creates increasing agitation in the crowd as his commanding voice turns shrill. *Good.* I think they should be panicked—*all of them.*

The orange glow is slowly coming closer and closer, and now I can hear the soft cackle that has come to haunt my dreams every night.

. . .

This epic disaster started out so small, as all disasters do, I suppose, with one seemingly insignificant action that ignited the chaos. I only noticed things getting out of hand when it was too late. I remember the day this whole mess started so vividly.

. . .

I feel my phone ding in my pocket. I pull it out, hoping my brother is texting me that he is on his way. Ed is late *again.* Instead, it's a number that neither my phone nor I recognize.

Unknown: Hi.

That was all it said—a simple "Hi." Yet that one word changed my life.

Me: sorry, I think u have the wrong number

The user texts back instantly, sending my heart racing.

Unknown: I assure you, I don't.

Me: I'm not sure I understand. Who r u?

Unknown: Someone you don't know now but will VERY soon.

I block the number immediately, choosing to trust my gut, but another text pops up using a different number.

Unknown: You can't get rid of me that easily, *Rosalynna.*

This is the precise moment everything starts to spiral out of my control. I look around, suddenly getting the feeling I am being watched.

"Get in." I jump out of my skin. A scream of absolute terror ripped from my throat. "Chill, it's just me."

I sigh in relief when I realize it is only my brother.

"You scared me," I scolded. My heart is still beating madly in my chest.

"Duh," Edward said. He is making a dumb face. I slap him lightly on the arm as I climb into the car.

"You goofball," I say, laughing a fake laugh that dies on my lips quickly. Ed's face turns serious. Killing the car's engine, he focuses his full attention on me.

"Something's bothering you," he says. "What is it?" I look at him in mock disbelief.

"Come on, spit it out."

"It's nothing. I have a test I need to study for." He gives me a dubious look but leaves it alone. He notices me starting to trace circles on my thigh with my fingertip.

"So...you don't want to get Starbucks?"

Even though I know he is trying to distract me, I play along.

"Are you kidding me? Of course, I do!" That makes him smile, a smile that is so rare these days. Edwards's smile is contagious, and soon, I am grinning, too. All my worries about the unknown texter shift to the back of my mind.

"Then let's go," Ed says, twisting the key in the ignition, causing the car to rumble to life.

I walk into my room, my cup still in hand, ready to restart my work. I sit at my desk, examining the circuit board for what needs to be improved. The entire product is built, but something internal is stopping it from working. My hands fly across my machine, twisting and tightening certain things until I am confident it will work. I insert the motherboard, pulling and turning the screws, and then I flip the switch on. The shield whirs to life, a seemingly holographic film coming out from the center console—

. . .

"WATCH OUT!" I am shocked back into reality by Edward's voice.

I turn just in time to see a fireball whooshing towards my face. I jump to the side, but not as fast as I should've. The fireball scorches the side of my leg. I let out a scream of agony.

"Rosalynna!"

"I'm fine," I call in the general direction of where Ed's voice came from. "I need you to hide before you get hurt."

"Not without you, I'm not." He has always been protective, but even more so since our parents died. This time, I am trying to protect him.

"Please, I need to know you are safe so I don't have

to worry about you during the battle we both know is coming." He doesn't utter another word, which I take to mean he has found a safe place to hide—out of the way and out of sight.

"Oh, Rosalynna," coos a voice that sends chills down my spine.

"Ernaline," I grumble through gritted teeth. Stepping out onto the road, I notice it's clear. I send a silent thank you to Ed for ensuring everyone else was safe before he found safety. Although, I could kill him for not finding a hiding spot sooner. A little voice whispers in the back of my mind. *You'd be dead if he hadn't stayed out and warned you.* I hate the fact the tiny voice is right. But before I can curse myself further, Ernaline's white flowing hair comes into view. She blocks the sun and pins me with her glowing, almost otherworldly, green eyes.

"Let's end this once and for all!" I call up to her.

"No thank you. I quite enjoy tormenting you," she says, a hint of a chuckle hiding in her voice. I grit my teeth and aim my laser gun at her, preparing to make the first hit. I look down at my leg...second hit. Noticing my movement, she sprints out of firing range and responds with her own personal gust of fire.

The fight has begun.

But I need to switch to my shield before I can shoot. The force of her fire pushes me until my back touches a rough brick wall. Finally, able to regain my footing, with something stopping my backward trajectory,

I shoot off multiple blasts. She avoids them with annoying ease.

"To your left!" cries an unrecognizable child's voice. As promised, a new, bright, hot stream of fire is heading from my left. Ernaline used my distraction as an opportunity. I shift my shield so it is at an angle, blocking both streams of fire coming from each of her hands. I strain with the force of it. *Your back is going to make you pay for this later.* This new defensive position also leaves me unable to shoot in return. Ernaline approaches closer, an unsettling smile spreading from ear to ear.

"What were you saying about ending this once and for all? Because to me, it seems like you are the mouse trapped in the corner, not me. I'm the cat. So I'll give you a choice. We can stay here, with you blocking my fire and sending pathetic shots all day, until you finally tire, and I win. Or, you could surrender right now, and I win."

"Never!" I scream. I try to make eye contact so she can see the resolve that burns in my eyes at the prospect. My shield slips at the attempt to look at her, and fire instantly streams my way.

"Either way, I win," she says smugly, pushing her flames onward. They inch closer and closer to my body. I can feel the heat singe my arm hair. I look around frantically but can't find a way out. I swallow the lump of fear in my throat and hold my chin high. *At least I'm going into death with some semblance of pride.*

"No!" Ed hollers, running out of his hiding spot, causing a distraction.

"No!" I echo as Ernaline's flames turn towards Edward and hit him full in the chest.

I dash over to him, no longer caring what Ernaline can do to me. I fire shot after shot at her as I run. I barely feel the sting of the fireballs she sends back.

My mind is running with the horrifying possibilities of what will happen if Eddie dies. He is the only reason I am alive, the only reason I haven't been put into foster care. I reach him and crash onto my knees, barely registering the pavement that scratches at my skin. His clothes have been burnt to a crisp, and I can smell the burnt tissue and blood. The more I look, the worse it gets. I can almost see his big heart beating in his chest, all of its protection *gone*.

He looks up at me with a smile but pain in his eyes. My selfless brother, who adopted me and kept me out of foster care, is still trying to show me he loves me, smiling through the pain. His head drops back down to the pavement. I quickly gather his mess of soft hair, now thoroughly coated in sweat, in my lap, attempting to act bravely but failing.

Rubbing his head like he used to do for me when I would have a nightmare, I plead, "No, Ed, please no." Tears stream down my face, blurring my vision.

"Hey, I'm okay. I'm fine, see," Ed says, weakly trying to stand but not even managing to hold himself up on his hands. I let slip a sad smile. Even while he's dying, he is trying to act strong for *me*, like he's always done.

"Promise me you won't leave."

"I promise," he whispers as he takes a shuddering breath and collapses back onto my lap, blank eyes staring up into the sky, no longer filled with the joy, life, or kindness they held only moments before—a trickle of blood pools from the sides of his mouth, signaling massive hidden injuries as well.

"No, no, no," I mourn as unrelenting sobs rack my body. *Why hasn't Ernaline attacked yet?* The little logical voice in my head prods. I turn, unable to see through my tears, but my feet know what to do better than my brain or heart. A blaze awakens within me as I stand, burning brighter than I thought possible, fueled by my fresh and ever-expanding grief. I look up; my eyes reflect the burning city around me, which mirrors the fire ignited within. My internal fire expands.

Looking up, I see Ernaline has been preparing. A giant fireball now sits in her hands. When Ernaline and I lock eyes, she sends it flying. I can't dodge out of the way quickly enough. It hits me square in the chest, knocking me backward and onto the pavement. The wind is knocked out of me, and pain explodes through me. I lay helpless in the road, in agony, and gasping for air, as fireball after fireball is sent shooting towards me. *Do Eddie and I have matching wounds now? Will we both die the same way?* Blackness claws at the edges of my vision. The last thing I see before pain and exhaustion drag me entirely into blackness is Ernaline's face of triumph.

. . .

He is here, waiting for me. Eddie is here! I survey where we are. It looks like we are in a tunnel, but we aren't. We are on a road. Ed stands at the beginning of the road and sweeps his arms in a welcoming gesture, allowing me to go first.

"C'mon sister, let's go find peace." The meaning of his words hit me—we are both *dead*.

Chapter 3

Rosalynna

4 weeks later...

My fingers weave a wire through the mechanics in the back of the holographic shield I'm working on. I hear a giggle.

"You look so stupid when you concentrate," Ed barks a laugh behind me. The sudden sound causes my fingers to misplace the wire, causing a spark. I yelp in pain and suck my thumb to soothe the hurt of being shocked. This only manages to make Ed laugh harder. I glare at him as he leans against the door frame, doubled over in laughter.

"You jerk!" I shout, barely able to hide my laughter. His eyes crinkle in the corners. He is holding back tears from how hard he is laughing. His face is almost as red as a tomato, and his lips are tinged a slight blue from lack of oxygen.

"I-I'm s-s-sorry," he gasps, but this time it isn't him.

He still holds all the characteristics and charm of himself, but he has shifted. His lips aren't blue because he is laughing so hard but because he is dying. Ed may still hold all of his normal characteristics, but the light of his eyes is gone. He lays in my lap, dying from wounds delivered while trying to protect me. I have failed him. The light from his eyes slowly fades, as does his laughter.

. . .

I awake with a gasp, attempting to sit up but can't. I am forced back down by the sheer weight of my pain. Every corner of my body hurts. I try to remember how I got here, but the last thing I remember is Ernaline's triumph and then my dream where I was dead. My eyes feel raw, like sand has been rubbed into them, and my throat feels like I have screamed to the point of drawing blood but no sound. I try to assess my injuries without causing further pain, but it is impossible.

I hurt *everywhere*. Once again, I try to sit up but nearly black out from the pain. Without the ability to move, I retreat further into my mind.

I remember my dream, although it seems more of a nightmare now. My heart is crushed once again by the weight of grief. Hot tears prick the back of my eyes, allowing some relief from the feeling of sandpaper against my lids. I let the soothing tears fall. That pain is replaced by one I am sure will never heal.

My grief consumes me. I feel like I have been crying for hours. But still, tears flow in steady streams down my face. My eyes are red and puffy, my face sticky and covered in snot, but the tears won't stop. It feels like all the liquid in my body has come out in tears. I should literally be a shriveled husk of a human rather than still alive and breathing...and crying while I have failed my brother. *I have failed. I have failed.* The phrase continues on a loop in my head. Failure pounds so hard into my brain that it has branded itself into my soul. *I have failed. I have failed. I'm a faliu*—I am interrupted from my thoughts by a door opening off to my left.

"Good to see you awake."

The slippery voice sends a familiar feeling of terror through me. I sit up immediately, but the pain is unlike anything I have ever experienced before. I feel like I am sinking into white-hot tar, quickly losing consciousness. The last thing I see is the floor rushing up to greet me. But I am stopped by an unnaturally cold hand catching me and whispering, "I can't have my daughter dying. Now, can I?" Then, I sink further into the tar of pain and nothingness.

Chapter 4

Rosalynna

Five days later...

When I finally manage to emerge from the sludge of pain, everything is fuzzy. My surroundings are unfamiliar, and I can barely move without wincing in pain. I close my eyes to concentrate on what happened and how I got here. It all comes back so fast the air gets knocked from my body. Tears spring to my eyes, but they don't last long, as I suddenly remember the last words I heard before I fell unconscious. *"Daughter."* But that can't be possible. My parents are dead.

. . .

I am standing over their coffins, bawling my eyes out. They were too young to die; their lives snuffed out before their time. Their faces were barely recognizable, covered in cuts and bruises that would never heal or fade. My father was buried in a somber black suit, and my mother in her favorite yellow dress. At least the worst of their injuries are covered. They had always loved to dress formally, using every excuse they could to dress up. I'm so angry at myself. I am already thinking of them in the past tense. I am mad at how easily I slipped into the reality they are dead. I start to rub circles against my thighs, something I always do when I am anxious. My thoughts wander back to the crash.

. . .

That disastrous day was full of fun and joy. It was my birthday. We were on our way home from the funnest day of my life. It was my 16th birthday, and we visited my favorite dinner spot—Timmy's Diner. The dinner had been full of laughter and stupid dad jokes. The memory brings a small smile when I think about how my dad always turned everything into a joke, even if it was serious, and how we tolerated it and sometimes found it funny. His jokes were always punctuated with a laugh or smile.

The memory also brings sadness as I remember how my mother always thought my dad's "dad jokes" were funny, even when they didn't make sense. When my mom laughed, she always smiled her big toothy smile, showing off her slightly yellowed teeth. She was never embarrassed about her crooked or yellowing teeth, and when she smiled, her confidence and happiness would rub off on the whole room. Her smile could make a space glow brighter and put a smile on everyone's lips, too. That's how they managed to stay together for twenty-three years; they found joy in each other!

The fun had continued to the car. Ed had playfully shoved me into the car, causing me to bump my elbow against the side. I laughed while rubbing the tender spot. Ed's laughter filled the car. His laugh came from within, only capable of coming out when he was genuinely happy and found something funny. He was never able to fake a laugh because you could always tell instantly.

He continued laughing at the fight between our parents in the front seat while trading looks with me in the back. My parents were bickering because my dad had spilled some mysterious orange...something on his black shirt; the contrast between the two was striking.

"I just washed that shirt, and you got it dirty again!" Mom shouted. Her soft brown curls bounced along the road, her brown eyes narrowed in anger but crinkled at the edges in amusement, just like Eddie.

"I don't know; it just happened," my dad said, sounding clueless. His brown eyes widened in confusion, framed by his raised eyebrows, which resulted in his entire face comically stretching. Ed and I were both laughing at how mad my mom was and how stupid my dad looked. Dad shot Ed and me a look of disbelief before offering a sly wink. *He's figured something out.*

"Maybe next time you could be more careful?" Mom asks, sounding even angrier. At the same time, her outer shell cracks, revealing the mom, who could never stay angry for long.

"You're one to talk. You have yellow sauce almost down your entire front."

This was an overstatement. But as all our gazes turned to Mom, we saw he wasn't wrong. She did have a streak on the front of her light blue shirt, highlighting the stain even more. Her mouth formed an "O" of surprise. This only served to fill the car with more laughter.

"Look out!"

A sweet little deer had run into the middle of the road. The deer looked innocent, tinier than other deer in the area. Its tail flicked as a signal of danger. My big-hearted parents immediately swerved the car to avoid hitting the deer. As the vehicle swerved, it went out of control, hit the guardrail, and flipped over.

Blood. That's all I saw: blood and glass everywhere. A moment in time that had once been filled with laughter was now filled with screams. The dirty pavement I was sprawled across looked like a murder scene. My arm and leg felt like they were on fire. My arm was bent at an odd angle. I didn't want or care to see what had become of my leg.

"Mom! Dad! Ed!" I shouted over and over again until my throat was raw.

"Rosalynna!" Ed shouted somewhere in the distance. I managed to stumble up on my one good leg, dragging the other uselessly behind me, as I went to look for him.

"Ed!"

"Rosalynna!" I finally found him. He was covered in blood. I scanned him from top to bottom; lots of cuts and bruises, but no significant injuries jumped out at me. Ed smothered me in a hug that made me grunt in pain.

"Rosalynna? Are you okay? Where does it hurt?" he asked, his voice full of concern.

"Where's Mom and Dad?" I asked, ignoring the questions.

"I don't know."

Together, we staggered towards the front of the car. I was barely able to stand on my one good leg. My head grew dizzy and fuzzy from the loss of blood. "Lean on me," Ed said, his voice sounding far away. Finally, he noticed I was falling over my own two feet and tripping on every shard of glass. *There is glass everywhere!*

When we found our parents, a strangled gasp escaped both Ed's and mine throats. He let me go. I fell to the ground as he rushed forward. I tried to crawl to get to them. They were both hanging upside down, covered in blood. Mom's neck was twisted at an unnatural angle, an unsurvivable angle. An object impaled Dad. It was too coated in blood to indicate what it was. I looked away. But was still able to smell the metallic scent of blood mixed with the sweet smell of fuel wafting off my dead parents' bodies.

My birthday dinner threatened to come up the same way it went. I stumbled to the side, unwilling to puke on my parents' bodies. I felt a sense of revolution run through me at the word "bodies." Everything I had eaten was slowly rising in my throat, as the images of my parents hanging upside-down circled my mind—slowly burning itself into my memories and leaving me unable to ever forget.

I heaved and heaved until I was sure there was nothing left writhing my stomach. And even then, I didn't stop. My throat continued to spasm, causing my stomach to flip. I was now puking only bile. My body was wracked with violent motions. It felt like my stomach had flipped inside-out and was working its way back right-side in.

"You done?" Ed asked, rubbing my back.

"Yeah, I think I am," I said, panting. By this time, sirens were ringing in the distance, the scent of blood fading, and the adrenaline running through my body was waning. I fell against Ed, and he supported me.

. . .

Ed rubs my shoulder, bringing me out of the memory and back to the funeral before us. He must have noticed my nervous tick. He has always been able to pick up on it. Edward stands tall, tears barely prickling his eyes. I am in awe of his inner strength.

Along with helping to plan our parents' funeral, he is engaged in a court case for my custody so he can become my legal guardian. He is eighteen, only two years older than me. But he is so much stronger and more mature than I am. I am glad he will be my new parent instead of some random foster care provider.

. . .

The door to my left opens, jerking me out of my thoughts and fully into the present. The present where Ed is dead and I am not, and I feel overwhelmed with pain and confusion.

"Glad to see you awake," the familiar voice says. Though it is full of warmth, it sends chills of dread down my spine. It's the voice of Ernaline.

"Yes, well, I think you owe me some answers."

Chapter 5

Rosalynna

Ernaline sits down with an air of calm I can no longer possess. I attempt to sit up again but have to lie down. The attempt leaves me gasping in pain. Ernaline approaches me with hands that hold an unnerving coolness and surprising gentleness. She supports me, taking away most of the pain, as she helps me sit up. I am propped against the pillows that had previously engulfed me to help reinforce my back, neck, and head. She takes her place back in the chair, resting in the corner. Crossing one leg over another and intertwining her hands within her lap, she asks, "So, what do you wanna know?"

"Many things."

"Like?" Ernaline rolls her eyes.

"Where am I?" Taking in my surroundings, I blurt out the first question that pops into my head. I am on a small, yellow-stained mattress tucked in the corner.

The room itself is sparsely decorated: a chair in one corner, a mattress opposite that, and a door made of cold metal. Everything smells of dust, including myself.

"In a bunker far, far away from civilization," she says. Her calm, relaxed, collected demeanor never falters as she breaks into a strange grin. Her impossibly thin smile stretches from ear to ear, showing only a slight hint of teeth. Something about *her* seems unnatural and makes me uncomfortable. That grin tells you Ernaline has something on her mind. Something I am sure I won't like. The grin that only means terrible things for me.

"Why am I here?" I ask, annoyed by the vague answers.

"I need your help," her smile disappears.

"With what?"

"You'll see soon enough," Ernaline says, her voice full of calculation. "In the meantime, you need only focus on your recovery. Training starts tomorrow."

"Training? For what?" I inquire as I start rubbing a circle against my thigh. Anxiety is slowly creeping up my back, and no amount of rubbing is going to ease the shiver worming its way through my body.

"You'll see," Ernaline says, breaking into her creepy smile. Her smile leaves me in fear as she leaves. I'm afraid for what's to come.

Chapter 6

Rosalynna

I can finally walk again. My first steps are painful, shaky, and slow. I hold onto my bed for support; my knees begin to shake and threaten to buckle the farther into the room I get. I can only manage a few short bursts of movement at a time. Despite my slowness, exploring my room is easy because it's so tiny. The four walls that surround me feel suffocating. Not even close to the warmth that once filled my home. The gray-yellow tint from the overhead light fills the room with an ominous feeling. A white metal door stands in the corner to the left of my bed. My bed is small, shoved in the corner of the room, with only a single itchy pillow and sheet. It's slightly rumpled from where I had laid in it for...who knows how many days. Besides the door and the bed, the room is scarcely decorated; it feels more like a prison. *It is a prison.* A voice whispers in the back of my head. I turn my head a little and spot a sink, mirror, and toilet hidden behind a half wall for some semblance of privacy. I try the door, but it is locked. Yep, this *is* a prison cell. I let out a sigh of resignation. I am trapped in a prison cell. *What did you expect from Ernaline?* I scold myself. *She is heartless.* Ernaline has proven that time and time again.

. . .

I smile down at my new toy. After I got my shield to work, I immediately started on another project, never allowing my mind or fingers to stop. This time, I'm building a "laser pointer," as Edward teasingly calls it. *Sure, it's a laser pointer, but one that can blow stuff up, not just point things out.* Holding it in my hands makes me feel safe as if I could protect myself. The anonymous texts lurk at the edge of my mind, reminding me why I built this.

Ed returns to my side, "Ready when you are, Little Badass." I chuckle. After our parents' death, he has taken to calling me that instead of Rosie to remind me of how strong I am. Rosie, to my ears, sounded childish and weak. "Little Badass" makes me feel capable.

I take aim at the paper targets we printed out and stuck onto cans. I take my first shot and miss. I let out a breath of agitation. "Hey, it's okay. Go again," Ed reassured.

"Yeah, you're right."

"I always am."

I shoot him a look of mock annoyance while holding back laughter. He gives me a goofy grin, telling me he isn't buying it. That's all it takes; I burst out into laughter.

The feeling of laughter still sits in my chest as I aim again. This time, I hit the paper right on the outer edge of the target. The laser leaves a small burn mark where it had gone through.

"Hey, there you go, you're doing it!"

I shoot again and again, slowly getting closer to bullseye. Finally, I make it.

"Okay, now let's see how much damage you can cause," I whisper encouragingly to the machine as if it were a child. In a way, it is. I had created it and cared for it. But, before I could turn up the intensity, my pocket dings. I had gotten a text.

Unknown: Nice job.

Me: Leave. Me. Alone

I immediately block the new unknown number. *Again.* A prickle that I was being watched settles over my skin.

"Are you okay?" Eddie asked, sensing something had changed.

"Yeah, yeah, I'm fine," I say, shaking my head to bring me back to reality. I aim again, but this time, when I fire, the laser hits something just beyond the target as it sprints out of the trees.

Time seems to slow as multiple things register at once. One, the thing that had run out of the trees was a deer. Two, its neck was already dripping with blood from where its carotid artery had been cut. Three, it looked as if it blinked once in surprise before the shot from the laser gun incinerated it.

I gasp in horror as I realize what I have just done. The deer might've already been fatally wounded before I shot it, but my action definitively killed it. The small reminder of my parents' death brings tears to my eyes. Ed turns to me with a look of horror, which I'm sure is reflected on my face.

Something clicks in my mind. The unknown person responsible for the threatening texts is also responsible for this heartless and cruel act. They have been watching me for quite some time, and they know the fate of my parents.

. . .

I sigh and heave myself up to my feet, whining from the pain. *Steady.* I remind my legs as I will myself to do what comes next. I let go of my bed and take a shaky step away. My legs are wobbly and unsure of themselves beneath me. *Stupid, slippery floor, you're helping nothing.* Nonetheless, I take one step and then another, building my self-confidence step by step.

Smiling, I slowly make my way across the room. The pride filling me reminds me of the first time I had successfully ridden my bike.

. . .

I can't steer. My dad's steady and calloused hand stays firmly planted on the back of my bike to keep me going straight. We are going farther than we have ever gone before. My knees and elbows are covered in minor cuts from previous falls. He and I are giggling at the sheer thrill of how far and fast we are going.

"Go, girl!" Dad encourages, giving me a shove and pushing me forward. I whoop as I gain more speed than I ever have before.

"You're doing it!" Eddie shouts right behind me, though his voice sounds far away.

"Turn around," my mother chimes in, sounding slightly worried and panicky. *Moms.* I roll my eyes but obey. I awkwardly angle the front of my bike back towards my family to start a wide turn. A massive smile spreads across my face. I am doing it without help. I am doing it!

My family is laughing and hooting. I throw my arms up in the air in celebration. Promptly losing control of my bike, I swerve hard sideways. I fall onto the hard pavement, scraping myself up even more. The bike and I land in a heap. Ed immediately runs to me to make sure I am okay. But I can't stop laughing, giddy with my success. I did it.

. . .

I run into a cool and unforgiving surface. Looking down, I realize I have crossed the room with the help of my dead family egging me on. A faint smile curves my lips.

I turn on the cold water tap from the sink I had run into. Gazing at myself in the mirror, a disheveled girl stares back. My hair is tangled and matted. I run my hands over the thick white streak of hair that generally lays in the front of my head, framing my face.

Currently, everything is everywhere, making it appear like I have salt-and-pepper hair. My light green-grey eyes look haunted, and the dark bags under my eyes aren't doing me any favors. My already pale skin looks almost sickly. *I remind myself that's what you get for laying in bed for who knows how long.* I am still staring at my unkempt appearance when the door opens.

"Glad to see you up and about," purrs Ernaline. I shoot a look of pure hatred her way. I turn the water off.

"Can't say the same about you," I snort.

"Such hostility when I only come here to give you food. You must be ravenous; you've been asleep for nearly four weeks."

Four whole weeks. A whole month.

She pauses, letting that sink in.

"I advise you to eat something, no matter how much you hate me. I have big plans for you tomorrow," Ernaline says with a knowing smirk and a glint, making her otherwise dead eyes glow lime green.

As she leaves, she sets down a tray with a sandwich and water. The food looks like it has been set out to rot for a week. I look at it in disgust before a low grumble from my stomach forces me to walk over and eat. Much to my disappointment, I *am* ravenous, as Ernaline predicted. I eat the whole rotten thing. Within minutes, I have finished my plate. The sandwich tasted like cardboard and the water like ash, but it satiated my hunger for the moment. I sink into bed, my legs throbbing from use. I fall asleep with the taste of ash still lingering in my mouth.

Chapter 7

Rosalynna

My legs will not stop shaking as I follow Ernaline down a long, bleak hallway. I am slowly realizing how much of a prison this place is. There is scarcely any furniture, color, or other signs additional people live here. We finally arrive at the door at the end of the hallway. This door seems different; it is thicker than my or any other door I have seen in this desolate place. Ernaline opens it and signals me inside with a grand, sweeping gesture. Eerily similar to the way Eddie welcomed me into death.

The door is like a portal. Behind it lies a circle made of sawdust with high sandstone walls. After not seeing any color for so long, even this muted beige overwhelms me. Ernaline lets me gape at this seemingly new world, at least compared to my room and the rest of the bunker. The sawdust crunches beneath my feet as I join Ernaline in the center.

"Now, let us get to work."

"And that would be...?"

"You have to learn how to use your powers," Ernaline stated.

"My what?!" I question in disbelief. Ernaline looks at me with triumph in her eyes. My mouth hangs open as the realization sets in. *I. Have. Powers.*

"O-okay," I stammer, curiosity quickly overriding shock. "How do I use them?"

"Simply reach inside yourself, look for a kind of light or pool of power, and draw from there."

I close my eyes, trying to do what she has told me. It is much more complicated than I expected to look into myself. It feels like all the stupid soul-searching exercises they always make us do at school. I don't know how long I stood there with my eyes closed, not doing anything. I feel an intense heat brushing against my skin. I open my eyes to see Ernaline standing there with her hand on fire.

"This is taking too long," she states impatiently.

"I'm sorry. I don't know how to get there," I say with a hint of sarcasm.

"Maybe this will help," she says. The fire leaves her hand and comes blazing for my face, though it is moving slower than normal. I close my eyes again and quickly search for a way to protect myself. I can feel my heartbeat rising as fear, grief, and the memories of destruction Ernaline's fires have caused threaten to overwhelm me.

Suddenly, I am not aware of anything except

blackness and light. I don't know how I have gotten here, but I know what I am looking at. Power. *My* power. It looks like a raging river of pure light. I reach down to skim the surface and feel my body heat with electricity. It feels like all the times I have electrocuted myself, trying to tinker and build, rolled into one. I open my eyes, aware of where I am and the fire approaching me. I shoot out my hand to meet the fireball. But instead of burning my hand, the fireball is greeted with a blaze of lightning.

I feel like I am the pond sitting at the river's end, slowly filling with power. Ernaline smiles, that smile that doesn't quite look human but a smile that radiates accomplishment, nonetheless. The fireball explodes.

I did it, I realize with a burst of pride and shock! I am still bursting with electricity. I need to make it stop soon. I focus on creating a dam in my mind so the seemingly infinite power flowing from within me will stop. I close my eyes and painstakingly place each brick in my mind, cutting off the power. I sag with the energy it takes and open my eyes again. Ernaline's smile is replaced by a grim set of her jaw that looks as if it has been carved into the impassive stone sculpture of her face. I groan internally, somehow knowing I'm not done yet.

"Good, now follow me. We have a lot of work to do." *Yep, I guessed it.*

An armada of gadgets lay before me. "I want you to use your electricity to power and then use them,"

Ernaline commands, standing there waiting for me to start.

A feeling of giddy excitement floods through me at the prospect of being around machines again. They have always been my friends, more so than people have ever been. I nearly run to the table, wanting to welcome the familiar feeling again. I must settle for a fast walk since my legs can't keep up yet. They are shakier now than before I used my powers.

I arrive at the table feeling of a sense of familiarity, excitement, and happiness. My fingers start working before my mind can even catch up. It feels like all the happy days I had spent training and tinkering with Eddie by my side.

I aim for a target set on a wooden beam. It reminds me of an archery target. I close my eyes, slowly finding my way back to the river of power. This time, I remove a small portion of bricks to allow the energy to flow and to fill me again. As I let a slow trickle of electricity flow from my fingertips into the motherboard, the machine whirs to life. I pull the trigger, and the target explodes, wood fragments flying everywhere. I duck to avoid losing an eye. *I need to turn down the power.* I scold myself. Adding bricks back into place reduces the amount of energy I can access. Firing again, I make a small, smoking indent rather than demolishing the wooden target. *Progress.* The air fills with the scent of smoke, reminding me of all the good times I went camping with Dad. We would always make s'mores. Before bed, he would dump water on the campfire, always lecturing me about fire safety. *Ernaline must've never had that talk.*

"Very good," Ernaline purrs.

We continue like this for a very long time. Ernaline coached me on how strong or weak I should make the flow, eventually increasing the distance. My body is slowly becoming weaker, as is the power and intensity of my river. The more powers I use, the closer my body sags to the ground. Finally, I crumpled to the floor from pure exhaustion. Ernaline rolls her eyes and mumbles, "It must be the human in you."

"I'm sorry, what? What do you mean by 'the human in me?' I *am* a human."

"Not exactly. You're half human, half Widdlepuff."

"What's Widdlepuff? And how do you know this?" I ask, not entirely comprehending what she is talking about.

"Widdlepuffs are an alien race, much more sophisticated than yours. And I know all this because I'm your *mother*. And I am a Widdlepuff."

My mind whirrs. I can't believe this is happening. Her saying I was her daughter before comes back to me in a flash, emerging from the fog of pain it had fallen into. I didn't dream it. This is real life, or whatever semblance of real life this is. My mind is a scramble. *I have powers that I got from my alien mother?!*

"This can't be happening."

"It is happening. Your adoptive parents *are* dead. But I am here for you now." I stare at her in disbelief, thinking a million questions all at once.

"I'll explain everything later, but only after we've taken you to your room to rest."

A sudden rage fills me. Why is she caring so much about me now, after all the terrible things she has done? Why would she do such terrible things to her daughter in the first place? I am too tired and confused to bottle up my rage, as usual, so I just let it explode.

"Why do you suddenly care? You had no problem hurting everyone I love!" Instead of responding, Ernaline walks away. "So, you are running away now! I see how it is! Well, screw you!"

Ernaline comes back, but this time with a wheelchair. She lifts me, acting like she hasn't heard my remarks, and places me in the chair. "Where are we going?" I ask, still seething but also silently glad for the wheelchair's support.

"Your room," she states simply.

We reached my cell, and she helped me to my bed.

"Now, give me answers."

"As you wish," she sits in the chair across from my bed. "It all started when I tried to take over my home planet."

"Wait, so you really are an alien?" I ask, testing out the strange word. I blame my slow processing on all the physical and mental trauma I have been put through.

"Yes, and so are you, well, half-alien."

"Back up, what!" Even though she has already told me this, it feels like brand-new information. Again, sleeping for a whole month really messes you up. I can't stress this enough.

"I'm getting there. If you would stop interrupting me, I could explain it to you."

"Right, sorry," I murmur sheepishly.

Glaring at me, she says, "If you don't shut up now, I won't tell you.

"It all started when I tried to take over my home planet. As you say here, long story short, I failed and was banished to Earth. That's when I met your father. He was a sweet guy, and we fell in love fast. He was my first love. He got me pregnant, and nine months later, I had you. So yes, you are half-human and half-alien.

"Your father broke up with me before we found out I was pregnant because he found me too controlling," she says with a roll of her eyes. Widdlepuffs mate for life; we are simply not designed for a broken heart. This made me vow to stay focused on my true destiny —not the false destiny I built in my head with your father at its center.

"You looked so much like him that it broke my heart every time I looked at you. To protect my sanity, I dumped you on the steps of the Huxleys, whom you consider to be your 'biological family.' In fact, they were just the first family I found that looked like you. And, well, you know the rest."

I sit in stunned silence once she has finished her story. My brain is reeling from the amount of information I have learned in just one day. Even though I had been adopted, my parents have always treated me as their biological daughter. I'm curious if Eddie knew the truth. Despite my curiosity, the question settles again.

"Why do you suddenly care so much now?"

"Because you're my daughter, and I need your help."

Chapter 8

Rosalynna

"Now, I'll leave you to sleep." With that, Ernaline gets up and leaves.

"Wait," I call out. Ernaline didn't turn around or even pause for a moment; my voice didn't faze her. I sit back, trying to process everything I have learned today. Uncomfortable truth number one: I am half-alien, half-Widdlepuff. Uncomfortable truth number two: Ernaline is my mother and needs my help. Uncomfortable truth number three: I have powers.

My thoughts reel; I feel like I'm about to explode. I look at my reflection in the mirror with new eyes. The white streak in my hair is precisely like Ernaline's full white hair, and my eyes are simply a muted version of hers. I really am her daughter. The proof is staring me in the face.

I lay back down and tried to sleep. I want to forget the pain of losing Eddie, the shock of everything revealed today. I want to forget everything that hurts; all my memories, even the happy ones, are tainted with grief and pain.

Sleep never comes, so I retreat to my river of power —though now it has turned into a creek. I focus my attention on the dam. I am determined to make it easier to access my power. I remove certain bricks and replace them with a door. Now, I have a way to open, close, and filter in power without doing much mental work. After completing it, I finally drift off into a fit-ful sleep plagued by memories that are slowly twisting into nightmares.

The door opens, and I awake with a start.

"Now, I think it's time you help me."

"No. Good morning. How did you sleep? Just straight to business."

"I don't see a point in useless small talk when what I've been waiting for, for years, is suddenly so close." I sigh, accepting that I am still a prisoner, no matter what I have learned.

"I seem to remember you needed my help."

"Yes, I need you to power a machine." I am taken aback by shock. I don't know what I expected, but this seemingly simple task was not it.

"What is this machine for, exactly?" I ask suspi-ciously.

"To take over the world." Whelp, scratch the simple part of her ask.

"Wh-w-what?"

"You see when they banished me to Earth, they gave me another, unintentional, chance to rule."

"No," I state simply. My voice is steady, even though I am shaking with fear on the inside. Ernaline wants to take over the world, and she wants me to help her. I nearly explode with laughter at the absurdity of it all.

"You have two choices. Either join me willingly or don't, but then this will get very ugly, very fast."

"Never."

A cool chill settles over her, and a slow smile spreads across her face. The smile hints she is either excited or disappointed about what will happen next, but I can't tell which. "Then I guess we're gonna have to do this the hard way."

Chapter 9

Rosalynna

My palms are sweating. Ernaline's face stays impassive as she waltzes towards me, only a tiny glint of excitement hidden in her eyes.

"Are you sure?" she inquires.

I start to rub a circle against my thigh. My insides shrivel as the wheelchair is brought back over, and I am lifted into it. Ernaline is surprisingly strong for how gangly she appears. I heft myself out of the wheelchair, and even though my legs shake, I can still stand.

This time, however, she does not want me to have free will, and she pushes me back into the chair. *Is this what she wants to do to the entire world: take away their free will?* I speculate.

"Yes," I mutter in answer to the question from before. Even though, deep down, I know saying no wouldn't matter. By refusing Ernaline's earlier offer, the course has been set.

Ernaline pulls something out from under the bed. It looks like a box. She pulls exactly four things out. I squint to see what she is doing, nerves tensing throughout my body. She is holding zip ties. She secures me to the chair, tightening the zip ties around my wrists and ankles until they nearly draw blood, causing me to wince. *I can no longer escape.* The fact settles within me like concrete.

I am forcibly wheeled out of the room, and some of the tenderness that Ernaline held only moments before is gone. We turn in the opposite direction of the training room. I attempt to gulp down the lump that has formed in my throat. It doesn't work. We come to a door; Ernaline opens it.

It is a torture chamber.

My eyes widen in shock. Chains hang from the ceiling. A table of knives and other instruments, I don't want to think about their utility, sit along the opposite wall. A small candle burns in the corner, filling the room with a sickly-sweet-smelling smoke. Ernaline sets to work.

If she has a torture chamber sitting down here, what else could be hidden behind those doors? I shiver in dread. Even though I can't, my finger itches to start rubbing a circle against my thigh to calm myself down. The thing that scares me more than the instruments is how giddy Ernaline seems at the prospect of torturing me.

She turns her attention to me again. "Now it's your turn."

"My turn for what?" I am puzzled and anxious, and my voice is shaking and cracking with the strain.

"You'll see." With that, she cuts my zip ties. She is again lifting me into the air. She seems less sturdy this time, almost like she wants to drop me. She places my hands into the chains, securing them tightly above my head. The pain makes me cringe as the metal rubs against my slightly raw wrists.

"Don't be afraid," she coos in an *almost* motherly voice, misinterpreting my flinch of pain as a symptom of fear. *Yeah, right. You have a table of knives. It's very calming.* She practically skips over to the table.

"It has been a long time since I've done this. Now, where shall I start?" she muses. "I can't completely incapacitate you; you must still learn to use your powers and help me. So I mustn't do anything permanent."

"You don't have to do this," I try to reason with her. My fear is mounting; the metallic taste of adrenaline coats the back of my throat. She has done this before, and what I am about to endure will not be pleasant.

"Will you help me willingly?" she asked again. At that moment, I decided that I couldn't possibly help her, no matter what. Any hints of doubt disappeared the moment I was wheeled in and saw the chains hanging from the ceiling. She is no longer capable of caring about anyone but herself and her own selfish, destructive desires.

Ernaline will stop at nothing to take over the world,

and I know this from her unrelenting pursuit of me. And from the dark gleam in her eye whenever she talks about her home. I can't help her. I am sure that if she did succeed, it would be cruel. She will destroy other families if she is successful. Even though my family is dead, they are why I am the way I am. The kindness they taught me is still in my heart. I won't let her take away others' kindness or hope. Human's capacity for kindness is part of what makes us human.

"Never!" I hiss, determination coursing through my voice.

"Then there is your answer because you are the only one who can help me. Trust me, I've tried others, but you're the most promising." No other words are spoken after that.

Ernaline turns to me again, this time with a knife in hand. She walks closer, slowly, as if savoring the fear on my face. She brushes the knife against my skin as if in a tickle, but there is nothing sweet or funny about the gesture. It is all a threat—a final warning.

I clench my jaw tight, grinding bone against bone, fighting against the urge to squirm or pull away. She smiles at my grim determination and then presses harder until blood flows to the surface. I grit my teeth to keep from screaming. She does it again and again. She is trying to break me. But I don't.

Eventually, I start to sag against the chains, causing them to dig deeper into my wrists. I wish I were sitting in the wheelchair again, even if it makes me feel weak. Instead, she continues to cut. Scraping up the first layer of skin causes a new wave of pain I didn't know was possible.

She walks away, and I let out a sigh of relief. But this time, she returns with a serrated knife. This time, I can't hold back my screams as I feel the terrible blade rip through my flesh. The blade bears down on the already exposed pieces of tissue. She continues, but the more blood she draws, the more my vision turns into a tunnel. That's when she stops when I am hanging between consciousness and unconscious: life and death. A whiff of blood finds its way to my nose. *My blood.* That thought makes me want to pass out even more, if only as a temporary escape. Ernaline takes a step back to admire her work as if my mutilated body is some kind of masterpiece.

"Now, will you join me?" she asks, triumph already filling her voice.

"Never," I say in a near whisper.

"W-what?" Ernaline is clearly taken aback. But, taking a moment to steal herself, she continues, "Then I guess we have to move on to Plan B."

I am terrified of what Plan B could mean. I can't take any more of my blood staining the floor. *At least it adds a splash of color*—my delusional brain jokes. Looking resigned, Ernaline unhooks me from the chains, and I crumple to the ground. She signals me to follow. I attempt to stand, but my knees buckle, and I crash back down to the floor.

With a sigh, she continues to walk off. I crawl across the floor, smearing my blood everywhere. I heave myself into the wheelchair and slowly roll after her. With an annoying smirk, knowing she has won an unspoken battle of wills, she takes over the wheelchair.

We turn down a hallway I had missed the previous day. A steady beeping fills the air as we approach a room at the end of the hall.

This room was different. It had a glass viewing window, and the beeping got louder. It looked like a hospital room, and the bed was already filled with a patient, *Eddie*.

Chapter 10

Rosalynna

I stare in complete disbelief. Eddie is alive. He is *alive*. Everything stops for a second as I process what I am seeing. Ed lays on a bed, unmoving, looking practically dead. However, the constant reassuring beeping from the numerous machines he is hooked up to tells me he is alive. A tube is stuffed down his throat, causing a steady whooshing as his chest rises and falls. The dusty smell in the rest of the bunker is replaced with the scent of antiseptic solution. He looks more or less ghostly; his skin is nearly as white as the sheets he lay within. In this condition, he is not living, but he is alive. He's stuck between life and death.

A familiar tingling sensation settles down my neck. My heart beats faster, Ernaline is watching me. She wears a gloating smile, spreading unnaturally wide to reveal her teeth. This particular smile makes her look predatory.

"Wh-wha-why?" I stammer out.

"May I present to you Plan B," she says, ignoring my previous question.

"Why?" I repeat.

"I need your help."

"How?"

"After rendering you unconscious, I went over and revived him. He's in a coma for now. Who knows if he still has any brain activity? But I have won nevertheless."

My mind goes blank. My brother is in a coma because of me. *Is that a good thing or a bad thing?* I'm pretty sure that Ernaline's involvement is a bad thing. My quick elation at seeing Eddie one more time turns to dread.

"Why?" I repeat, unable to comprehend.

"Oh, dearie. 'No' is simply not an answer I am willing to accept. I had to make sure you would cooperate with me. I have simply waited too many years for my uprising. I've been biding my time, waiting for you to grow and develop your powers properly. I figured he would be good leverage if you needed additional persuasion. Through my observations, I've noticed your strange connection with this...human."

"Yeah, 'cause he's my brother," I scoff, anger filling me. "I will never work with a maniac— no—psychopath like you! Who not only kills my brother but brings him back to this...this torture between life and death. He doesn't deserve this."

"No, no, he doesn't. I suggest you work with me."

I feel like my heart is filled with lead. I can't help her, no matter what. I look away from Eddie's unconscious, mostly dead, body. I can't look at him when I answer, "No." A look of disbelief fills Ernaline's eyes before she masks it, her calm outer shell quickly returning.

"Very well, you always pick the hard way," she hisses. A button suddenly appears in her hand. She presses it with a sly grin directed at me. The room is suddenly filled with alarms as Eddie's breathing and heart rate quickens. A buzzing sound accompanies the cacophony. Edward's limbs and head jerk as an electric current runs through him.

"Make no mistake, he does understand pain."

That is my breaking point. I am so shocked and horrified I barely register what Ernaline is saying.

"Stop! Stop! Stop it!" I scream. Tears soaking my face as I watch the nauseating sight continue before me.

"Not until you agree to work with me."

I am engaged in a battle with myself. I have to save Eddie; he hasn't done anything to deserve this. But I can't help her. I *need* a plan. The beeping increases, and I know what I have to do.

"Fine. I'll-I'll help," I grimace. Immediately, the alarms stop. I watch Ed's heart and breathing steady. Eventually, he lays as he had before, as still as the dead, once again.

Ernaline smiles self-satisfiedly as she wheels me back to my room. I try to remember where we were and how to find him again, but my mind is running through everything that has happened. When we arrive back at my cell, I am still lost in thought.

"You've been quiet. Are you okay?" Ernaline asks, that motherly tone back in her voice. But the question has evil intent behind it. I stay silent, trying to think. Unfortunately, my mind focuses on that question. I don't know if I am.

I lay on my bed staring at the ceiling. My body aches from all the cuts and bruises that mark me as Ernaline's masterpiece of pain. My heart aches with the pain of the guilt I carry. I replay everything that has happened today; I was tortured and then had to watch my brother be tortured because of *me*. In a flash, I know the answer to Ernaline's mock, concerned question. *No.* I am not okay. I don't know if I ever will be again.

Chapter 11

Rosalynna

Screams fill the air. I can't tell where they are coming from. I look around. Everything is black, almost blank. The screams themselves are unsettling and constantly changing. At one point, it sounds as if they are excited, like little children getting candy. Then, they shift to ones of terror—the sounds of people running from a house fire. A chill runs down my spine. I feel unsettled like I am being watched. The screams are coming closer. A cackle joins the chorus of screams—Ernaline's haunting, mirthless laugh.

I go deeper into my mind, trying to open the door to my power, urgently feeling the need to protect myself. The door is more challenging to open than usual, and it feels like I am not completely in control. Maybe this isn't real. The screams turn shrill, the laughing louder, making my ears feel like they will explode. I need to escape.

All at once, the screams turn eerily familiar. Like the screams, Ed let out when he saved me. His screams are now running on repeat, sometimes being warped. I wrench my mental door open and send a wave of electricity through the darkness. Eddie is illuminated, lying there in the dark, looking helpless. The images flicker between, when I left him dead in the city, to him laying in the hospital bed. Both scenes remind me of him in my arms, apologizing. And both times, I can't help him.

. . .

My ears are ringing, and I am sticky with sweat. The room smells faintly of sulfur. Everything I own has been charred at the edges. Apparently, I really had used my powers while I slept. *Maybe my powers are unreliable.* I can't get the memory of Edward's body out of my head. I know I have to save him and stop Ernaline, and for that, I need a plan.

Staring at the ceiling, my mind runs through a million possibilities. I don't even know how to get out of here. But then, I remember something: the guns in the training room. They are similar to the one I made, and I am sure I can get them to work.

I stand up, resolve settling in my gut. Maybe I couldn't save Eddie then, but I can now. I will save Eddie and stop the world from being taken over by my mother. I just need a couple of supplies. I jiggle the door handle, expecting it to be locked, but I am delighted to find it is not. Ernaline must have thought I was so brutalized I wouldn't try to escape.

The training room is empty. Nothing from the

previous day is there. A burst of anger shoots through me. I let my power fire away at the targets. I concentrate on providing just enough power not to blow the roof off this place—which is also the right amount to blow Ernaline to pieces. I smirk, nearly laughing, giddy with the sense of action. I still need that gun in case my powers really are unreliable or can be used against me, but for now, I have something to work towards. I continue to fire shot after shot.

I trudge back to my room; everything feels heavy. I hear a faint thump somewhere. Ernaline. I sneak around, trying to ignore the protest coming from my limbs, as I crouch behind a door to watch. Ernaline is moving the guns to another room in her apparently giant, underground lair. I freeze in shock. What else is Ernaline hiding? I sneak closer. Ernaline whips her head around. Wincing as I dart back behind cover, it feels like everything is about to crumple beneath my weight. I definitely need a little more time to heal before launching my rescue plan. Begrudgingly, I quietly retreat to my bedroom.

I let out a sigh of relief as I sank into my bed. My body needs to rest, but my mind refuses to relax. I slowly weave a plan. It all hinges on that weapon. It is my only chance to fight against Ernaline. I can't avoid her fire. A shiver runs through me, remembering how it felt to be burned by her before.

Conviction strengthens my spine as I understand what I need to do. I dread it more than anything. I need to get close to Ernaline. To make her believe I have realized the truth of her words. I have to become Ernaline's daughter in earnest. I have to pretend to help her. It's the only way I can get Eddie and me out alive.

Chapter 12

Rosalynna

I stand, blasting wooden targets. My body aches from numerous cuts and bruises. The quality of pain reminded me of right after the car crash that took my parent's life. The more I blast away, the more my pain increases. Eventually, I have to sit down and retreat within myself to keep from passing out from sheer exhaustion. I lean my head against the smooth wall behind me, wishing I could have a tree at my back instead of wood and metal.

The sawdust begins to move around. I opened my eyes to see Ernaline standing in the middle of the training room, looking slightly impressed at my progress. Numerous targets are singed or completely smashed from where I lost control. *Now's your chance. Pretend you need help. Pretend that you are going to help her.*

"Impressive," Ernaline makes eye contact with me, signaling towards the targets.

"I can't seem to get the right amount of power. It's either too little," I point to the slightly burned targets, "or too much." I point to the spots where targets should be but sit on the floor in pieces.

"All you need to do is reach within yourself and focus your power like a laser, increasing its distance and strength. You should be familiar with lasers, considering you burst a deer's head open with one." My face shifts to one of disgust as she brings up the memory, showing she has been watching me for longer than I thought. *Maybe not just watching, but also doing?* She must be the mysterious texter, the one who ignited the chain of events that led us both here.

"O-okay," I say, stuttering over some of my words as I realize how long she has been stalking me.

I close my eyes and try to follow Ernaline's directions. A feeling of deja vu washes over me—an eerily similar feeling to the first time I used my powers. I open my mental door, barely more than a crack, trying to make my powers laser-like, just as Ernaline taught me. I fire at the closest target, burning a perfect circle in the bullseye.

A new smile appears on Ernaline's face at my success. This smile is not one of cruelty, malice, or even plotting but indicates she might be proud of me. In some little twisted corner of my heart, something similar to love starts to bloom for this woman— alien —who somehow, amongst all the evil, also has a sliver of motherly compassion and pride. It's been so long since my own mother spoke to me, and I desperately miss that connection.

"You know, you remind me a lot of my sister, Ambrosia. She was always so full of determination."

"What happened to her?"

"I slit her throat to take the throne." I stumble back at that confession. That warm feeling from a minute ago evaporates instantly. I need to stay focused. *Here's my chance. I need to try to meet up in her office.*

"I would love to hear more about your family."

"Why?"

"If I'm helping you, I would like to know more about you." This was all a lie.

"Of course, but not here; it smells like sweat and dust. Why don't we go to my office?"

"S-sure," I nod and follow her out. So far, so good.

Chapter 13

Rosalynna

I sit in Ernaline's office, trying not to squirm. *You have to do this.* I remind myself for the umpteenth time in the approximately two minutes I'd been waiting.

I look around the room, still slightly shocked, to see her office is furnished. It has a bookcase with titles that read *Rumble in the Jungle, Our Inner Demons, A Wish, Death Ride, Ghost, and Home.* A red rug that mimics the color of blood sits under my feet. *I'm not sure if that is an intentional choice, but it's very sinister chic.* My stomach lurches at the thought of just how many had spilled their blood for me. I push the thought aside, scolding myself for nearly spiraling. I need to stay calm and focused. Candles are everywhere, making the room smell of smoke and throwing warm light around the walls. Another door stands to my right, where Ernaline vanished a moment before. I sit in a cushy leather chair that seems to swallow me. I like it. It is cool under my skin, soothing most of the pain, both mental and physical, earned from both my torture and training.

"Care for some tea?" Ernaline inquires, jerking me out of my thoughts.

"Y-y-yes," I stutter, trying to dislodge the lump in my throat. The hot tea feels centering as I try to gather my thoughts.

"So, why did you want to talk to me again?" Ernaline's tone sounds almost as if she genuinely cares, like how my mother used to ask how my day had been. Steam from her tea briefly covers Ernaline's pale face, nearly erasing her features and allowing me a second to act like Mom had never died and that *she* was actually the one sitting across from me. Offering me tea to calm my nerves about a test she knew I'd ace, even if I didn't believe it myself.

"I wanted to get to know you better since you are my-my," I pause, willing myself to say it. *For Eddie*, I chant, *for Eddie.* I seal my eyes shut and flinch inwardly to hide my reaction to the next word, "Mo-mother."

Ernaline's eyes grow thoughtful. "I see-" she trails off as if losing herself in her past. I almost feel bad for her as pain and sadness pass over her face. "What do you wanna know?" she finally asks, returning to reality.

"Why all the candles?" I blurt without thinking.

"The scent is comforting to me," she shrugs simply.

I am taken aback by how this monster can feel or even needs to feel that emotion. It reminds me how alike she and I are, how human she can be. Then, my mind shifts to a bigger focus.

"You said that I am half alien."

"That's right."

"Remind me, what's this alien race called?"

"Widdlepuff," she states matter-of-factly.

"What are they like?"

"We are not much different from you humans, but far more intelligent. We also far outlive your tiny life-spans. I'm 109 and middle-aged. We have explored every inch of our galaxy, finding wonders you couldn't imagine."

"What else?"

"We mate for life. When Robert broke up with me, it was something I had never heard of before, let alone experienced. The feeling of heartbreak overwhelmed me. I thought we were destined for each other, like I said. I decided if I couldn't have my soulmate, I might as well console myself with world domination." That far-off look returns to her eyes, a faint smile tainting her lips.

"You are lucky we haven't taken over your world yet. There was a king who was killed because he tried to expand the borders beyond our home planet. That's how my father came to be crowned. But I guess if the Widdlepuffs had taken over Earth sooner, things wouldn't have aligned for me to meet Robert. And I would have missed my opportunity to rule

Earth on my own. With your help, of course." An unknown warmth spreads across her face, softening her features. I squirm uncomfortably at how strange the emotion looks on her.

"Do you know what killed your parents?"

"A-a car accident?" I say, taken aback by the sudden change of subject.

"No, a big heart. That is why you agreed to work with me; you lead with your heart, not your brain. You got that from your adoptive parents. They also led with their hearts, not their heads. It's why they swerved and died instead of hitting the deer and letting one, among millions, die. That's also why Eddie sacrificed himself to save you. However, I would have simply incapacitated you, not killed you. You are far too important to die." I let that sink in. It had a ring of truth, of horrifying truth.

You still need to get the gun, a little voice whispers in my head. I had gotten lost in my thoughts and feelings for Ernaline, just like she said, more heart than head.

Something strange bloomed in my chest, an odd sense of compassion and pity. I was slowly realizing that Ernaline wasn't exactly a villain. She was just *broken*. Abandoned by those whom she loved.

Maybe that's why she made me shoot the deer's head instead of the target. She was trying to make me stronger and more like her. I scolded myself. I needed to stay on task.

"Can I have more tea, please?" I asked, attempting

to get Ernaline out of the room. Even though I hadn't finished mine or even really started, she didn't seem to notice. It just shows how lost Ernaline was in her memories.

"Huh? Oh yes, sure," Ernaline says, returning from her thoughts. However, the nostalgic, far-off look in her eyes doesn't leave entirely.

She exits the room, and I immediately spring into action. I searched the little sitting area for the boxes I had seen the previous day. I find one in the corner, tucked away like she is trying to hide it. The box rustles as I open it; wincing at the sound, I look over my shoulder to ensure Ernaline isn't there. The box seems to glow with hope. I grab the gun and bolt. The first step is done.

Chapter 14

Ernaline

17 years earlier...

"Need a hand up?" A handsome stranger stares down at me. He is offering his hand. I am hesitant at first to take it, but his light gray eyes hold a foreign but comforting emotion— compassion. I take his hand, offering him a smile that feels strange on my face.

"My name is Robert," he says, returning my smile. He shyly brushes his hand over his brown hair, swiping it from his eyes.

"I'm Ernaline. Thank you."

"Ernaline, what an unusual name."

"Thank you?"

He smiles again at my confusion. My stomach feels like it is full of butterflies. A low growl of hunger quickly replaces the fluttering sensation. I take a step back, afraid of how he will react. Instead, Robert offers me a sheepish grin. "Care to come with me to get a coffee?"

"That would be wonderful," I return his sheepish grin. Oddly, I am all smiles with Robert. Considering my entire life is upside down, this is unexpected.

I sit across from Robert in a small coffee shop. A croissant is in front of me. I poke it with a fork, unsure of what to do with the strange, flaky object, a pastry, as Robert calls it. Seeing my reluctance, Robert reaches over with a fork and sticks the strange object in his mouth.

"Delicious." Crumbs drop out of his mouth. I laugh, the sound foreign to both my lips and ears. The fluttering feeling is back. Robert looks down at his hands, suddenly nervous.

"W-would you like to go out again tomorrow night?"

"Yes." I offer a bright smile.

. . .

That was the first of many coffee dates. Robert continues to treat me kindly without hesitation. Some small part of me is secretly suspicious of the un-questioning compassion he continually demonstrates. *Does he want something from me?*

Still, I allow myself to get wrapped up in him. I am changed from who I was on my home planet. With no sister to compete with and no promise of power to warp my priorities, I find the parts of me my father fearfully rejected begin to fade. Robert's love is so freely given, as opposed to the love skimpily shown to me growing up. Some small part of my heart begins to change. A sense of kindness starts to flourish. Instead of just receiving the love Robert gives, I can now return certain parts of it. I like this feeling—the feeling of being nice.

. . .

Showing compassion to Rosalynna through the simple act of making tea and answering her questions reminds me of the love Robert once offered. But Robert made his choice and so did Rosalynna. I can't let this pass.

Chapter 15

Ernaline

16 years earlier...

"You can't keep doing this!" Robert screams at me.

Robert is fed up with me, to say the least. After the first year of our relationship, he began to lose patience with me. His kindness changed me, but I can't seem to escape the impulses of my upbringing, even though I really do try. Often, when he does something kind for me, I treat him with suspicion.

He has given me a beautiful necklace. The necklace is full of pearls shaped like a flower. I took his gift and responded with a simple question, "Why?"

"What do you mean why?"

"Why give this to me? What do you want?"

"Nothing. A smile?"

"So now you're trying to control me!"

"No! I would never do that." Robert takes a step

backward. I am shocked by the look of genuine disbelief on his face.

"You know what? We are done!" He thunders.

"What? No, you can't!" I plead.

"Exactly, *you're* trying to control *me*," his expression shifts to anger. "We're done. I'm breaking up with you!"

"Breaking up" is an unfamiliar concept to me. At first, I didn't understand what he was talking about. I thought pieces of he or I were physically breaking apart. Ultimately, that may be easier to deal with than the metaphorical piece of my heart he takes.

Widdlepuffs mate for life, typically through an arranged marriage, hardly ever for love. I thought Robert and his love were my new destiny, like the throne was my old destiny. Robert breaking up with me, severing our bond, is a cruel act. Much like when my father disowned me. I feel bereft, cast aside.

Robert takes the part of my heart that holds the capacity for kindness. All that is left of me are the parts my father saw and rejected: jealousy, selfishness, a thirst for power, and a deep capacity for cruelty. I am restored to my former self, but I am *broken.*

Robert showed me the power of kindness but also the coldness of heartbreak. It feels like love itself has controlled me. Despite his protests, he made me more like him, more human, and more easily controlled. I smirk as a new idea takes hold.

What if I controlled all of humanity? Humans easily do this to themselves in more ways than one every day: love, politics, money, fame, and cruelty, to name a few. I know cruelty very well. If the part of my destiny with Robert has collapsed, then the part of my destiny to rule shall rise.

Chapter 16

Rosalynna

Present day...

Coming to a halt in a hallway not far from Eddie's hospital room, I admire the gun in my hand. Slowly, I open the door in my mind, letting a little power trickle through—the familiar whir of a machine engaging thrums under my fingers. I gently squeeze the trigger and plant my feet to keep the blowback from flinging me against the wall—the gun fires. I smile, pleased. I hear a little noise from the office Ernaline is in. I look backward, fear coming over me.

I run. My legs burn. Soon enough, I reach my room. I am out of breath, and my heart is beating painfully against my ribs, but I am safe. I hear no noises or foot-steps behind me and let out a sigh of relief. Sinking against the door, I clutch my chest and let calm wash over me. *I did it, Eddie. I will save you*—a silent promise but an important one.

The memory of Eddie lying motionless brings a sudden burst of anger. It spreads through my veins. I punch the mirror, which shatters, sending shards flying all over the floor. My hand is bleeding; I hiss at the pain. I gaze at the broken shards scattered around the floor. They still reflect me, but this time, they are *broken*. It feels like a reflection of who I am on the inside. I look away, unable to bear the thought of what Ernaline has done to me, is doing to me. Remembering the feeling of care and pity I had towards Ernaline seconds ago, my mind twists, and I can't decide who I should trust or blame and *why*. I am so confused.

Pushing those jumbled thoughts aside, I stare at the glass on the floor, and another idea comes to mind.

What if I make a knife? It won't hurt to have a backup plan if the gun breaks or something goes wrong. I pick up the biggest mirror shard and notice a bit of blood from where I had punched it. I start looking around my room for anything I can use to fashion into a handle. I pull a strip of leather, a band of metal, and a block of wood from underneath my bed frame. I tie it together with a single zip tie from the box Ernaline had stored there. Smiling to myself, I calmly start to sharpen the glass against the metal. It helps me focus my thoughts and hone my plan.

I am going to shoot Ernaline in the leg, or both if need be, to immobilize her before I destroy her world-domination machine. Some weird part of me that acknowledges she is my birth mother won't allow me to kill her, even if it would be easier to shoot her in the heart and run. Perhaps she will live to find the good, loving parts of herself again.

Then, I will save Edward. He deserves my very best effort; after all, he has been my entire family, both brother and surrogate parent, for years. We will escape together after he wakes up. Then, we will live our version of happily ever after. I smile at the thought of living peacefully with my brother without the dark feelings of grief or fear hanging above our heads.

I hold up the knife in front of my face, admiring how the edges reflect in the dim yellow light. That'll do. I feel a slight sense of pride at this rudimentary weapon I crafted.

I have always been brilliant. "Special" or "gifted" is what everyone else called me. I was the smart girl who always had her head in a book. I lacked friends, but Edward has always been there, and that was enough for me.

I used to tinker for fun. Eventually, I started making more complicated things like guns and shields to prove I could do it. But I have never made something as rudimentary as a knife. I chuckle. *They used knives in the caveman era. I'm a cavewoman—hear me roar!* I have a plan in place and three weapons to complete it. I am going to escape. All I have to do now is wait.

Chapter 17

Rosalynna

2 days later...

"It's time." A voice says behind me, jerking me out of my thoughts.

"F-for what?" I question. I had been watching Eddie's steady heartbeat and breathing, willing him to wake up and escape with me.

"To finally finish what I've been waiting for! You and I are going to control the world." Adrenaline runs through me. *No, no, no. I have nothing on me! No, wait, I have the knife.* Even though the thought is meant to soothe me, it only causes me more stress. I will be at risk of being blasted with one of Ernaline's best and only weapons, her fire. I had been hit with it once directly, and I had nearly joined my brother in death. Fortunately, neither of our deaths had stuck.

I'm moving. I didn't realize I had inadvertently

started following Ernaline. I need to pay closer attention to our path so I can make it back.

The room we are going to is the farthest of them all. My legs start to burn. We are heading slightly uphill towards the surface. It'll be easier to control everyone that way. Easier access to the surface means a thinner barrier between the bunker and the ground, allowing the signals to control humans to have better transmission. I hate that some small part of me respects the fact she has thought this out so thoroughly, and it is, in fact, a good plan. Ernaline gestures to me through the door.

I let out a small gasp. The machine takes up most of the room. Somehow, even just sitting there inert, it fills the air with a sense of malice. The Frankenstein-esque machine is made up of pieced-together scrap metal, wires, cords, and buttons. Some of the pieces are rusted, and others look as if they are brand new. The sight of it terrifies me. It seems impossible that it even exists. This one machine has the power to change the entire course of human history. There will be a time before the machine and a time after—free will versus no free will.

I stand there in shock, my limbs entirely frozen in place, except for my finger, which had begun to rub circles on my thigh. I can't possibly imagine I am the key to making it work. Ernaline shoves me from behind, forcing me to stumble into the room on shaky legs.

"Let's get started, shall we." It's a statement, not a

question. I can't think clearly. All I can process is that I am being pushed closer and closer to this thing that feels like it could be my end. Ernaline forces me down into one of the seats.

"Are you ready?"

"No."

"No?"

"No. I can't do this. I refuse." I finger the knife sitting inside my pocket. The time to act is now. I lunge, knife in hand, as a smile morphs Ernaline's face into one of grotesque horror.

Chapter 18

Rosalynna

A fireball comes straight at my face. I change tactics and fling open my mental door to let my powers flow. I stop the fireball with a bolt of energy. She pushes harder. Her powers have developed much more than I remember. I need to get close enough to disable her with my knife. I know I can't keep this cat-and-mouse game going for long. I need a new plan because my original plan won't work. The makeshift knife is in my hand, ready.

I cut off my power and duck. Ernaline is shocked when her fire scorches the opposite wall instead of me. I lunge and graze her leg with the dull end of my knife. I curse silently, knowing I must go hand-to-hand with her again. I have to immobilize her legs and maybe even her arms to keep her from killing me.

She turns around and throws another fireball my way. It grazes the side of my leg. I grit my teeth to keep from yelling out. She shoots another one, hitting my leg directly. The smell of charred clothing and...I can't finish that sentence without puking.

I launch myself at her again. My vision blurs at the edges, narrowing to Ernaline's leg. My whole world narrows to that precise target. I stab it. She lets out a noise somewhere between a gasp and a shriek of pain. I try to sever her Achilles tendon to prevent her from walking.

She whips around and creates a stream of fire aimed at me. I have to roll quickly to avoid being blasted. I roll directly onto my knife, producing a shallow cut on my stomach. *You are so stupid; don't cut yourself*, my ironic voice says. I nearly scream at myself to stop talking. I need to focus to make it out of here alive.

I lash out again, this time managing a cut to her arm. I can't tell if it has slowed her down or not. I strike out again. I nip her in the other leg. She crumples. Her fire stopped at some point, but I just now notice. I make one more incision, ensuring she will barely be able to walk, let alone follow me.

A sharp pang of regret runs through me. "I'm sorry," I attempt in a cracking voice hardly above a whisper.

I finally peel myself up off the floor. I try to put pressure on my burned leg and nearly join Ernaline on the floor *again*.

I drag myself out of the room, holding the machine of horrors. I rely on my memory and navigate towards where Ed's room is. In my weakened state, I am grateful for the decline towards his room—my leg throbs to the rhythm of my heartbeat.

I hear an all too familiar beeping only Eddie's room holds. I ram into the door and bounce off. I wasn't expecting it to be locked. My shoulder stings from the impact, and I rub it to soothe the sharp pain. I send a bolt of electricity to melt the lock. Now, the door pushes open with ease. I pause at the threshold; Eddie looks almost dead. Him, but not *him*. It never hit me how much life he held before. I slowly approach him and squeeze his hand to let him know he is not alone.

His heartbeat stays the same, and my heart sinks ever so slightly. I quickly unhooked him from the nodes that had sent the torturous electricity through him before. For the first time, it dawns on me that I have no idea how to wake him up. My plan never included a wake-up step. *What if I pull the wrong plug, and he dies?*

"No! I can't think like that!" I blurt aloud, needing to hear the force of it. I need to figure out a way to wake him up. I consider jolting him awake, but then I remember: I just removed all those electrical con-nections.

Pacing around the room, I consider and then elim-inate idea after idea. Finally, seeing as I have no other options, I disconnect him from all the machines. I start with the IV bag, thinking it could be dosed with something to keep him asleep. I remove the needle from his arm and stanch the drop of blood with my finger. I rub his arm, willing him awake. His skin is cold to the touch, reminding me of how Mom and Dad felt when I held each of their hands before they were put into the ground. Next, I disconnect his breathing tube from his mouth, not wanting him to choke on it when he wakes up. His heartbeat slows.

"No!"

I send a tiny shock of electricity from my fingertip to his heart. His heart begins to beat steadily, but it only lasts momentarily before it starts to drop. I do it again.

"You've got to hang on. Please, hang on for me, your little sister. Please, hang on for your Rosie." I revert to my childhood name, "Little Badass." I don't feel like a badass now. Instead, I feel weak. Remembering my nickname, that only he used, causes more tears to spring to my eyes. His heart slows again, and I reluctantly accept the truth.

We both aren't making it out of here alive. Eddie is dying. In fact, he has been dead for a long time.

This time, when his heart starts to slow, I let it. I rub his hand, reminiscing about all our time together and wishing for more.

I laugh through my tears when I recall his 10th birthday. He had gotten cake all over his face, and I mocked him for looking silly. Then, he smeared cake all over *my* face, saying, "Now we both look silly." We were covered in cake by the end of that party, and our sides ached from laughing so much. That had been my favorite birthday ever. Now, he is nineteen and dying. His humor, his protectiveness, and his zest for life are dying with him.

"Goodbye, Eddie. I love you. And I'll see you in another life or the next. One without pain or grief, one where we will find our happily ever after." Pausing, I think better than to say goodbye, knowing the promise I have just made. Instead, I settle for a simple "I'll see you later."

His heartbeat is barely registering anymore. I finally let the tears flow freely, unable to hold them back any longer. This isn't fair. Eddie doesn't deserve this. His only crime is being my big brother. He is the best brother in the world. And his heart has stopped beating.

Chapter 19

Rosalynna

I hear a sound coming from outside the door. I look up on instinct, but I'm not processing what I hear. My insides feel numb. Tears still stream down my face.

I see the trail of blood first. Ernaline. She hasn't given up. I passively watch her inch toward me. She is dragging her injured legs behind her. *At least you did one thing right today.* A tiny voice whispers in my head. I nearly laugh at the cruelty of the day, even though laughing seems impossible at the moment.

"Do it," I state.

"No."

"Why?"

"Because you are my daughter, and I won't kill you." It is eerily similar logic to what I previously concluded. But instead of relief, I feel anger.

"You've taken everything from me! Now, you won't kill me and let me join the only family I have. Which, oh yeah, you killed!" I stand up from my seat, an inner fire pulsing through me now, only to sink to the floor in pain. "I can't even walk properly because of you. Everything bad that has ever happened to me is because of you! And yet, and yet, I still don't hate you or wish you dead. But I can never help you either." My shoulders slump with the weight of it all.

"You don't hate m-me?" Ernaline's voice cracks, revealing just how human she has become.

"No, I don't."

"But I can't let you leave; you already know too much." I nod solemnly, accepting the reality of the situation.

"Then we fight."

With that simple line, a war starts that both of us will lose.

Ernaline sends a jolt of fire as I begin moving. The fire approaches me before I can process what I have done. I roll out of the way, the fire scorching my already blood-soaked clothes. I can't tell if it has burned me or not. I try again; this time, I am ready when Ernaline sends another stream of fire my way. I counter with my river of electricity, pushing back with all my might against her powers.

Ernaline is weak from blood loss, so my powers quickly overpower hers. She jerks backward, and I make my move. I grab my knife, which I have somehow managed not to lose in all the chaos. I hold the sharp end against her throat, pinning her down with my hips to keep her from moving.

"Will you let me leave?" I demand, even though I already know the answer.

A feeling of resignation buries itself in my heart. I know what I need to do. *You'll finally get your revenge.* One voice argues. *No, you won't.* Counters another voice that sounds just like Eddie. *She doesn't deserve to have her throat slit; she deserves your compassion.*

"I can't."

"Then I'm sorry, and I love you. *Mom.*" Even after everything she has done to me, I understand the truth. It was because she loved my father too much and couldn't deal with her broken heart that she made so many catastrophic decisions. She loved *too* much. She deluded herself into believing she was only leading with her head and not her heart. Despite her twisted lessons, I learned what I needed. I can't help but feel bad for her.

I regret what I am forced to do next. Ernaline's last smile crosses her face as I plunge the knife into her gut. It is an act of mercy and of last resort, not an act of revenge. Blood starts seeping out of her wound; her breath grows labored. She looks peaceful like she is glad I am the one to kill her. I led with my head AND my heart.

"I'm proud of you. My daughter. My Rosalynna." As Ernaline stops breathing, her final words resonate: she is proud of me.

I send one more bolt of electricity through the metal handle of the knife. My obligation is fulfilled, even if I had to kill the last person I have left in this world.

Another tear escapes my already swollen eyes. I sit against the wall, panting, looking at the bodies I have killed. Eddie is already cold, long since passed into the afterlife. Ernaline, though, is still warm. Her white hair lays limply plastered to her face. I shove my own white stretch of hair out of my eyes. I watch as her already paper-white skin turns ashy and waxy.

I have to get out of here before I puke. I try to stand again, but my legs are throbbing. The adrenaline has finally worn off. Letting the pain and exhaustion seep in, my eyelids grow heavy, and I let myself sink into a fitful sleep, not knowing if I would wake again.

Chapter 20

Rosalynna

I don't know how long I slept. I woke up feeling stiff, but in the same place I fell asleep— surrounded by my dead family. Still, in a haze, I get up and stumble-run out of that room, filled with people I have loved. I run through the bunker, past the training room, torture room, and finally, past the cell room I spent most of my time in, before realizing there is no exit that way.

I turn back and run towards the room that started this domino effect. Finding the machine room, and I destroy the evil creation. Sometimes using my hands, or my powers, in the end nothing remains of the machine, or my knuckles.

Exhausted but relieved, I find an access door in the ceiling that leads to the outside world. The bright sunlight hurts my eyes. I smile, happy to be alive and away from that awful place. I don't know where I am but hear cars in the distance. Ernaline had lied. *No surprise.* I was, in fact, *very* close to civilization. I pull myself entirely above ground and into the sunlight. I am standing in a field full of tiny flowers smelling of honey. Half-walking, half-stumbling, I move towards the sounds of civilization.

I have a funeral to plan.

Chapter 21

Rosalynna

Standing alone, I lower two empty caskets into the ground. The sun shines brightly in mockery upon the entire desolate and depressing scene. I couldn't even bring myself to find the bunker of horrors again to retrieve their bodies. I lay the body-less caskets of Ed and Ernaline next to my adoptive Mom and Dad. My memories of them are enough. All their lives were taken far too early and far too brutally. Tears swim in my eyes.

Everyone passing by looks upon me with sadness, confusion, and pity. I am quite the sight. My leg is still in a cast, and my knuckles and arms are heavily bandaged and stitched. I'm more bandage than skin at this point. People assume I have been in some horrific accident, not through actual hell.

The funeral director finally covers the caskets with dirt. I sink to my knees and cry, reflecting on the simple actions that brought us all to this catastrophic end. They both died because of me. Eddie, trying to save me, had ended up dead— twice. Ernaline, refusing to give up on her idea of destiny, forced my hand. However deranged, she thought of me in a motherly fashion. I still feel conflicted about my role in her death. However, I am still alive.

Ernaline had been right; a big heart had killed my adoptive parents and my brother. But my thinking side had killed her. I wondered, someday, which would kill me? My big brain or my big heart?

Chapter 22

Acknowledgments

Lilly Loar

I need to figure out where to start this. So, I'm just going to take my best shot. To begin, I am most grateful for my mom's help. She has been the one who has always encouraged my love of writing from a very young age. My mom has sat and given me countless criticisms and edits. I write and edit the way I do today because of her. She has been the one to sit and brainstorm with me when writing this. I could not be more grateful to her for her love, support, and all the work she put into this.

Next, I don't know if this counts, but my parents together. They encourage me and help me push to publish and print books. They support my writing even though I'm an amateur at best.

This next thank you goes out to both of my middle school language arts teachers. They have been among the most encouraging people to share my writing and my stories. Mr. Wood has read over this and has forever gushed about my writing. Mr. Atherton has allowed me to share and given encouraging reactions and excitement. Both of them said I should publish my writing, so here it is.

My most supportive friends are Leia and Isaac, who listen constantly and sometimes provide productive thoughts.

I may be forced to write this, but my twin Grace says she deserves an honorary mention here, so I'll put something. In her own words, she has provided "emotional support." And she came up with a silly pronunciation of Widdlepuff. She says it is the only acceptable way, so here it is, her honorary thanks.

To any classmate who clapped at the end of a story I shared, you have no idea how encouraging that was and how much it filled my heart with joy to see people enjoy what I create.

Finally, I'd like to thank you, the reader, for making it this far. I hope you enjoyed my story.

So, from the bottom of my heart and forever more,

Thank You.

About The Author

Lilly Loar was born and raised in Centennial, Colorado, and is proud to say she has survived middle school nearly unscathed. She is a voracious reader and writer of fantasy books. When not reading, writing, or talking about reading and writing, she enjoys performing in musicals, singing, taekwondo, hanging out with her twin, and traveling the world.

Ihsam with Flytographer |
Budapest